FOLLY RIVER

FOLLY RIVER

Wendy Salinger

Winner of the Open Competition
The National Poetry Series
Selected by Donald Hall

E. P. Dutton   New York

for Jill and Jennifer
and
Herman and Marion Salinger

Poems in this book have appeared, sometimes in differing versions, in: The New Yorker; The Archive; Green House; Sandlapper the Virginia Quarterly; Poetry East *and* A Duke Miscellany *(Durham, 1970).*

The poem No Children, No Pets *is based on the novel of that title by Marion Holland (New York, 1956, Alfred A. Knopf). The poem* Wind on the Moon *is based on the novel* The Wind On The Moon *by Eric Linklater (New York, 1944, The Macmillan Company). In the poem* Folly River, *"Molly goes to the Circus" refers to* Circus Time *by Marion Conser (New York, 1948, Simon and Schuster).*

For information contact:
E.P. Dutton, 2 Park Avenue, New York, N.Y. 10016

Library of Congress Cataloging in Publication Data
Salinger, Wendy.
Folly River.
I. Title.
PS3569.A45953F6   1980   811'.5'4   79-23058

ISBN: 0-525-10760-6

Published simultaneously in Canada by Clarke, Irwin & Company Limited, Toronto and Vancouver

Designed by Barbara Cohen

10 9 8 7 6 5 4 3 2 1

First Edition

CONTENTS

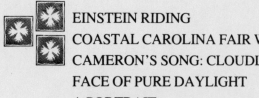

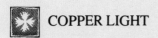 **COPPER LIGHT**

When the sun rubs the ocean in its oils,
and the banked cumulus is fired rose,
and the shrimp trawler rides

like a mythical city, white and lone,
when mullet crack the steel cover,
when I see the ocean in its fever,

I remember waking
from my own sluggish childhood
to the first bar of land.

SEASMOKE

On an island near this island
Poe blew on his fingertips,
red and stinging from the salt wind.
Was it the floaters
brooding in his eyes
or these white fibers
carded from the foam?
Forms steam
off the wet sand.
Tufts of spilt lining flock the air.
He saw the last palmettos lift
their gray trunks above the mist.
One by one their bristling
heads get taken
as if by Turner's brushwork.
Each thing wears its shroud.
Out where nothing is, a dog
barks at some discovery.

A man kneeling
nears me as I walk.
He crouches in the chemical smell of oysters
over his machine propped on the jetty.
The wooden posts, rotted almost black
and scrofulous with barnacles, suck the dregs
of brown tide like a drain

and wet his boot.
The hands that fit the motorcycle chain
are pale
with wedges of darkness under the nails.
The black jacket straining in the smoke
pulls up to bare his back
swirled with hair.
Orange wings are blazoned on the helmet
laid carefully beside him.
Gulls and turnstones skirt him
pecking for midges.
Their cries rust on the air.
I glide past him like the clouds of spume
that walk the beach.
Then I am once again turbaned in mist.
Then once again his dark machine materializes;
his blazing forehead, the red light in his wake.

He too is trying to get more lost.
His noise sputters before me
and goes out.
He thinks he can drop me off
in his cloud trail.
He thinks what disappears doesn't exist—
like a child craving the life of a hero or orphan—
he drives his deed into the cottonmouthed air.
He tightens his knees on the sweating,
metal flanks.
He thinks I can't follow him

into the cataract,
I can't hear
his feathery chest
or see the bird pulse move
up and down his rough throat.
He thinks he can be sifted
into nothing.
He is so restless
with the dream of rest.
He leaves me to the wind,
he leaves me blind.
Only this ectoplasm
is clear to the eye,
though I know the ocean
by its white noise.
Dim to everything
I meant
to walk
into the shadow of my own heart.

A ROOM IN NORTH CAROLINA

The ceiling paper was spiraled
with bluegreen florals.

Branches vexed the window.
Oh sick. They got in.

Tree frogs scraped the night.
Wistaria fumed in my throat.

One wall was vegetable,
one was animal;

but I confused their arguments
when it was late

(though there was a light
under the door)

and my name rose
at a pitch in both.

CHARLESTON, SOUTH CAROLINA, 7 P.M.

Vapors of musk and oyster rise,
a fine perspiring from the streets.
Blue bends toward purple:
a voice growing husky.
Things seek their silhouettes.
Green gathers darkness into the palm trees,
and the houses seem to rush out.
How whitely the stucco flowers and the pillar
that wavers as if seen through water.
So it is with consequences, the sun's aftertaste,
its resonances pool out in clapboard and stone.
Light hesitates between the streetlamp and the sky,
and distance is palpable as it is between those
who turn to each other with eyes downcast.

We lean from our bones but we don't leave,
we hang about, we hover at the edges,
we live in our mouths, heaviness on our tongues.
The tongue could do all the work tonight
of sight and sound and most surely of thought.
We hover at surfaces like moths
at our white linen, our moon silks,
at our own flesh. Surely under the fresh
ironing our genitals are cool and strange.
Surely they are fronds and gardenia flowers.

A weedy draft of ocean floods our lungs.
I know this now. How the past waits
coiled in an odor,
wet for the drinker of a limpid sound,
to be unbottled, to assail the blood.
I know the past exists.
And I could enter anywhere and find you, arranged
in the mime, for example, of just such an evening,
when lifting the cigarette through its steam
your arm inscribes forever that arc in space.
I know the rich molecules collect.

But who can court a balcony that commands
the bay to shine from its dark height?
My music's wrong, I'm not my own
bent low in the folds of a polished gown,
bowing to a man whose forehead shames the moon,
whose wrists flash steel.
A moisture films his formal lip
and sticks the shirt to the moving chest
and lifts the light on the beaded glass.
Is it possible that other histories covet us?

A stray dance can find our forms,
an incomplete gesture usurp our arms.
We shudder against the humid seizures
that wrestle us out of modern motion,
curve us, bow us,

wheel our waists through the watery air
where the ocean lives in its altered state
of brine and oyster musk, and smoke
from the factories braids with the swerve
of the black kids on their bicycles
who criss-cross the northend traffic.

TIME IN THE BODY AND TIME OF THE BODY

I think the buried beat at the dirt.
Violent hallucinations of azalea burst
over the gravestones. In the very dark
of a friend of mine, a spine
formed and bloomed.

I NAME

I name this day the Law of Harmonics.
I ring the palm's tine and it intones
the curve a crust of shore takes, the prone
sprawl of the pier, horizon that withholds
milky air from the deep blue sea.
The terns mew and spiral.
Mullet leap off-target, oh
in silver spasms.
When the porpoise vaults her sleek parabola,
when the pelican shoulders
prehistoric weight across my heart,
what should I interpret?
The wave that holds up light
sets my teeth together.

The horizon parts its line of far white cities.
A shrimpboat broaches shore, the crosspiece broods
the balance of justice on water, dips and drags
its nets of seaweed: the risen drowned.
At night encamped on black sky like the stars
her light is tuned toward yellow, a flesh tone nearer
than the diamond cold of space.
The palm frond's scabbard is a quarter moon
slung low between the wires, the fluid wires.
Hung so heavy with juice it beads
on the skin, the darkness pants.

I bake my bones to stone heat then down
them in the surf like laundry.
They're tipped with mercury, they taste
and ratio the fevers of water and air.
A fearful muscle curls at my neck,
spun force, tornado,
coil of brown and glint leashed, unloosed over me.
Bubbles of birdsong sprung from its throat
lapse in creamy eggwhite.
Distance stretches the net of light

insupportably. My tongue licks after a vast
vocabulary of texture. How my mouth lusts,
waters with a word (the word
is *almost*, the word is *almond*).
Oh I'd be a sop, a sponge
a photoplate for the finite
if I could make speech lie down
in the wash that laps the sand,
saliva under the tongue.

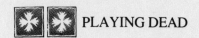 PLAYING DEAD

At age six: the dry taste of the desk,
head down on her arms, eyeballs pressed
to the black stars. Later she rushes into
the tall knees of a man. Wool and tobacco.
He lifts her where his glasses scatter
the light. She shouts, ''Ride to Montezuma!''

She should say, ''Home.'' She should lie down
behind the canvas blind where the sun pricks
through pinholes like the itch
of measles or scarlet fever.

The teacher too, her mouth tight, tight
gray curls, fiftyish beside
the child snug in the male scents
who escapes arithmetic.
By now she's burned or buried. I hope she burned.
How would the child know her, composed in earth,
brow, mouth, breast grown strange?

EUROPEAN STRANGENESS

The continent still dark when we docked at Le Havre
paled to a kind of ersatz dusk
before the sun swam up from the sea.
Our car rolled down the lower deck
and Mother sat inside and Jennifer and I
puzzled the sixteen pieces of luggage
into the pattern we trawled like a shell
over the olden dirt of Europe
and my father drew up the papers.

As if to focus and open the road of narrative
a man in a cap pedaled past and in a basket
strapped to the seat balanced his still life:
a winebottle, a burnt heel of bread.
And we too took the road to Rouen.
Plane trees like louvers calibrating the light.

My father talked of the hospital
where Flaubert's father worked and *The Dictionary
of Accepted Ideas* and how the bodies
stank through the streets.

He took his walk in the cobbled alleys
and Jennifer and Mother and I fell
into heavy, urgent naps and I dreamed
we went to Paris to the *Mona Lisa*
and I cried and cried until Mother asked
what was the matter and I said *beautiful.*
I woke as if a fever had broken.

If I thought of virginity it was in this way.
When you went to Europe you came back changed.
Even now I know how to love
the world as if it were unfamiliar
and I, who look there, uninterpreted.

It was the olive light, when we saw her,
not the smile, that I remembered.
The same light wet the trees
as we crossed from Belgium and the tumorous clouds
went slack over Holland like some torpor in my father
who had raged for an hour that we'd never learned German.
The light of Black Forests whose shadows are clocks,
whose floors are swept and laid with straw
where the hooves of the Prince arabesque to his castle.
How throttled my own growths were in contrast.

To be said in the words *North Carolina*.
Not in its name but in the cadence, a gravity,
something that sucks you home.
From the port of New York you tumbled down
into the part of the land that gave,
a muck of oxblood clay and kudzu.

His eyes too were thickly forested,
not like my father's abstract ocean.
And we were too much steeped in literature,
of that time when you read baroque as the kudzu,
indiscriminate, weedy, you don't know when you've stopped.
Oh we were embellished far beyond ourselves,

though I looked exactly into his eyes.
I'll never learn another form like his—
his adolescent, El Greco body.
I looked back into the leafy black,
past where the leaves complicate the light.
I thought I could enter like the light
that place so lush there is no
light, no light at all.

LETTER FROM THE BEACH

"The poet was filled with joy in being able to obey his parents."—FRANCIS JAMME

"Slow obedience is no obedience,"
my father chanted as we grew.
I live now where the days live
captivated by the Law.
But the light that lags in the wave
wrongs his tyranny.

THE FIRST FROST

With the first killing frost
they inhabit the walls. Mornings
the cat licks clean her fur and the small corpse
is stiff, already a museum-piece.

Then the truckload: the carcasses of deer;
the bucks floating dark, bare branches.

Well it is that time. The set table
brings us together another season.
The father carves, the mother serves
each daughter her portion.

NO CHILDREN, NO PETS

About the boy who cranked the carousel
all that summer in Florida
with sandy hair
and no father when the story began.
His three friends made a Dick and Jane and Sally.
Funny Sally, who hears it's hot enough
to fry an egg on the sidewalk. And so she tries.
She gets a chapter for calling hibiscus "biscuits."

All that summer a hot wind whipped the oleanders—
some white, some deep as burgundy.
The drops slid down the breastbone of the boy.
He crouched at his machinery, eyelids slit,
eyes a graying ocean. He had craft.
Jane and Dick and Sally fell in with him
when Mother was not at home. There was no
Father. When Mother moved in she was sly—
she joked at the sign "No Children," and the mean
old Landlady took it down like a useless spell.

Some afternoons they hung about the pier
and counted catfish the Negroes threw back.
"You stand still," the woman in the straw hat scolded
the whiskered fish while she baited the other line;
then: "Gimme ma hook, you bastid," and slit his throat.

Or shivered in the heat of the pavilion,
their hair gummed to their foreheads,
bare soles ginger on the concrete.
The smells were good and cheap:
popcorn and cotton foods
that gave them hangovers.
A dog threw up in funny colors.
Some papers scudded by
in a spasm of wind.
A few amusements ground in the dust—
he'd get them rides for free.
At night he hardly knew them where they stood
with Mother at his back bent bony with toil.

When August came the author made a storm
that cracked the dried palmettos and blew the boy
along like a piece of litter. At Mother's house
he helped them board the windows and trim the lamps.
When it got quiet they heard Mother's voice
rise in place of the wind: "It's only the Eye."
The wind came sucking harder at the chimney.
It rattled the locks like someone left outside:
He stood drenched at the door in the boy's eyes.
"Now we are six," Sally said in her way.
"Ever after," the author said, "Amen."

Didn't they know you might not ever come back
after the summer at camp? You might not fit
the cramped desk when September broke the hot
spell that held the world outside of time
and parents were born to bring the children home.

That even then the driver of the bus
might turn around in his seat, his face strange
as the pilot's in *Lost Horizon*, squinty-eyed
with the look of a far country.
That day they find the bus on its back in a ditch,
half-bedded in the rusty Georgia clay and the weeds
like the shucked crust of an insect.

MARRIAGE

In the apartment below me
two people are arguing.
Back and forth.
Back and forth.
The words, indistinct;
the cadences, familiar.
Back and forth.
I side with the woman.

All over the world
two people are arguing.
My parents are arguing.
If I'd never been born
I'd never hear such arguing.
But I'm the resolution of an argument:
I can't escape the proposition.
But it's true.
After the cups and plates
were put away, and the last
syllable extracted from silence,
they dug deeper.

Oh they're here again. Here at my elbow,
thrusting my hands to my ears.
Back and forth.
Be married? Be good? No,
no, cries the bastard.
Let the house
that always wanted to
fall, fall.

FOLLY RIVER

The river as pale
as *Molly Goes to the Circus*,
bluish and salmon

over the roofs and her father
comes to her room
when hardly a one is stirring.
(*Stirring* shifts the curtain.)

They talk strained,
not to wake the mother.
Time, he says, and

she hears, *Promise*.
How is it they do not break
even a saucer, but take
their shoes in their hands

and glide on socks
to the front step.
Here is the paper, left

by someone scarcely human.
Day is smoked glass
through which they pass
like motes.

Such a long time dreaming takes.
Long before the red sun and long after
there is a fitful scum on the water.

They ride the same wave home,
she on his shoulder, a
giant creature.
Candy on a stick, pink

as a sunset.
The sky holds no pallor
like the lamps of their faces.

Home the mother
has laid her special table.
But the child is too tired
and droops in her plate.

MUSIC ALONE SHALL LIVE

A blue so watered the sea might be the air.
Flat as ironing. Lapsed to a huge lake.
The sea might be the sky in its last bruised light,
blue as the globe, faint as if from wishing.
A water color so pale my heart goes out
where families bathe in fathoms of the sky
and walk in light that flows from the floor of the sea.
The sun sets in their slippery flesh.

Two black men and a white man in a white shirt
fish waist-deep, jump each wave that frills
with arms to the sky. The white man flips the rod—
a long tail, a heaving eel—above the lace
to save the reel. His good shirt is wetted to his back,
molded where the muscles dip to the spine.
He carries his stomach heavily before him.
It's too loud to speak. They mark the sky like sticks.
The hue of crickets stirs in the sea oats.

A father with a child at each hand like sand buckets
sways with the care of a tightrope walker.
The children lick the salt from their blue lips;
the light has them in a fever.
All the fathers, shy in their bare skins,

having let fall the bridles from their shoulders,
have come at last, in their weariness, to play.
By the hand he brings his children to see
the ocean he has worked so for and saved.
Each trio like this approaches the mountainous ocean.

In the grave light. So pale my heart goes out.
There is a longing so great it is nothing but longing.
It wants so, it wants more longing.
Far as the look of those who look on the ocean,
the light in their eyes glancing from the waves.
A look that rides the water and does not want
Africa but wants again and again
to pass like the ocean into its horizon.

At night the sea oats flash their dark blades
slick with spume and grit.
I wade to my knees
to see a boat kindle the water
like Cleopatra's barge:
a life just off-shore, where the rigging claps
the mast and stories drift
in pipesmoke with the night wind into the sea.
I watch its lights the way you'd watch a star,
staring so long you feel the presence of space.
I long for it, with it, like a listener
longing after a piece of music.

Boat, star,
anchor me in my longing.
All my life I am my own jailor.
Make me the watch;
take my shirt for your sail.

EINSTEIN RIDING

Could Einstein riding
his beam of light
save himself from falling

when he learned he saw
the world he loved
the way he loved it
because his eyes
traveled so at the gait of loving?

COASTAL CAROLINA FAIR WITH GAY BOYS

Those who never forget how to play:
which are they?
Oh
they know
how
to look lovely.
Prescient as women, they see
the image in another's eye.

Who keep alive
in waists and lowered looks
for me the older motion of a boy
who too disdained me in his most pure moment.
The shadow of his nose lay on his cheek
cast iron in the moon.
In his unsettled voice the wind
took place.

Who mount the constellations of machines—

                          the electric swing,
its cupola whipped and scrolled like bridal cake—

out and out and over the tents
of Jolly Dolly and Elastic Man
and Girl Alive who Has No Bones,
until World's Smallest Family dwarfs to ants,
far over the Four-Winged Duck, monstrous with flight;

each strapped in his bucket tight about the groin
and by a silver chain hanging on.

CAMERON'S SONG: CLOUDLESS SULPHUR

The man I work for hums a partial song,
or constantly clears his throat.
I think I will never forget his face.
It is pink and gray, it falls in folds.
He reads the *Supervisor* magazine at his desk.
He puts it away.
He checks these items under Raw Stock:
Kenmix, Ketone, Lithopone—names with no sex;
then: *Sulphur, Devil-A; sulphur Spider-J*.

Outside Cloudless Sulphur
butterflies meddle with the honeysuckle,
and a burnt taste drifts from the paper mill
or the oyster beds upriver.

The road ends in the factory.
It is school-house brick.
A semi with giant whitewalls parks outside;
it looks like the plant manager in spats.
The morning is blue, it disappears at seven.
His name is Cameron on the laminated badge
he flashes the guard at the gate. He came from the war

in 1946 to Building 5. Shipping and Receiving.
He worked for an old guy, he says.
I think, *Young Cameron*, to see him in those days
with his smooth cheek.
He fixes the coffee for the other men,
two pots a day.
Around the coffeepot they can't not joke
or whistle; they make trills,
but no tunes.

One song stops outside the warehouse door.
A man comes in. He is black,
in a suit of cracked silver,
his mask lowered and hanging about his neck.
He works behind the yellow danger signs:
Warning. Asbestos Dust. Authorized Personnel.
But the man tells me that it makes no difference.
For the dust isn't partial; it hovers, waits
for the supple cartilage in the nostrils, the fine hairs;
it settles in the porches of the human ear,
insinuates itself behind the fingernails
where the moon fades in their dark skins.
It sinks down with the breath
and on the staff of the chromosomes
finishes their song.

FACE OF PURE DAYLIGHT

I love you. Your face
is as clear to me as water.
I cup my hands, but
the water flows through them,
leaving the taste
of oxygen on my palms.

That's the way it is
when the first drops hit you:
that instant of air and water.
And how many grasp even that?

I can't hold back water
that wants to fall
anymore than you can keep
your light from the world:
I don't love you,
it's creation I love.

Oh if I could cup
your face, your fairness,
but it's evanescent, as much
like the soul as like water,
and I'm left with only
these weeping hands.

A PORTRAIT

for Lewis Hyde

I was thinking of the little cough
with which you scrape the back of your throat
before beginning some new project,
settling your tall knees under the table,
careful not to slop
coffee from the mug you set
between the aisles of print.
At your left a book of myths
and early studies of *dementia praecox*.
Neruda is at your head, and laid far to the side
the right hand, which you are trying to give a life of its own,
steadies the pen like an open boat with its oar.
Soon it will be moved to write
messages like "the hospital kiss,"
"the sea turtle, my desire";
soon you will write out "the limits of the language."

I could
raise each grain from the wood.
Your high face and the eyes
that are glassed in.
The hair tied back
that is fine and dark

as an Indian woman's.
How the sleeves are rolled
on the grayed white shirt
with the pleated front
and the almost clerical collar.
The forearm (the one
this angle exposes) fair
as the paper under it.

Once I thought your skin bloomed
lucid as milk because I had released you.
The grasses dipped from the wind and from
your giant steps; you took
the pitchfork you'd contrived to spear fish
in the Lake-that-speaks River for a staff
and let your hair loose like
a Jeremiah or a barbarian.
It was late. The light
no longer came
from overhead but instead
pulsed from the stones themselves.

Once more let me give you your existence.
I am so moved to study the act of love
in the descriptive light: how it recalls
things to themselves—you,
almost in the room, the abrupt
grating of your throat, how
you stroke your nose
with the big, furrowed handkerchief
as a sign you are ready
to begin your work.

THE DREAM WRITES

Sometimes the hands want. Only the hands.
To move out past the brain
like the hands of a sleepwalker.
Hands that led Mozart down the stairs
to answer the chord
that longed after him in the dark.

ASIA MINOR

A woman so beautiful it made me sad.
So white. Rose red.
Hair deep brown as a piano.
She took off all her rings before she played
and laid them there. And then she played.

THE POET ON HER CRAFT

I praise the serious talk of women,
two of us up all night creating the night.
How else to read the incline of a forehead
but that all ambition is a leaning forward.
I think we talk to some third thing—in need

of us, exceeding us.
(The map crawls after its cartographers.)
Oh yes the moon's a windowpiece: the china
egg she pitched from a ferment the room couldn't frame.
Now all of heaven's knickknacks glitter back

at her, in particular that porcelain smile
that's always pleased so much with its numinous lust
for objects. As a wave holds up the light,
the moon moves. The moon moves in the rooms
where women come to talk. The moon disturbs.

I know that piecework.
Carpentry of the invisible!
What is emotion without mathematics?
Mind is yeast to the night and sets
her tree flowering in a thousand white cones.

At eleven the husband takes to his bed.
Oh then the planes of her face put on their power,
the high bones vexed to virility.
So lightning betrays
the fine scaffolding of night.

Opal forehead,
black sky,
I invoke you.
Poem, my awkward
machine, we go on.

THE DISOBEDIENT PROPHET

Now we no longer speak
mouth to mouth;
but remember the old days?

How moist the word was
in me then.
Water that shaped to anything.

Did you grow jealous
when I too began to have adventures
that weren't mine?

Did you, who have everything
memorized, covet
my astonishment?

Remember how it was?
You used to say
thou to me.

With my lips
you cried out,
"Who's speaking?"

How I dread your return,
the flood
of creation.

WIND ON THE MOON

for Cynthia Keyworth

There was a story the night that Father packed
that Father told the sisters, dark and fair:
if they were very bad and a wind crossed
the moon when they were bad
it cast a spell.
This simply forced them to be very bad
and keep their eyes open.

First they ate: chocolates and dumplings,
plum cake, raisin cake, sugar and spice
cookies, plain cookies, unnamed pies,
until the Fair One sighed,
"I'm nothing but a Big Food."
The Dark One sighed. It was the last sigh
of content. It was the sound
a balloon makes, letting out.
They were both round in fact, in fact
the neighbor children mistook them for balloons,
or else were being vicious. They took sticks
and rolled them up and down hills.
"Ouch!" the Dark One cried, uncomfortably.

The girls were not popular.
This made them sad. And being very sad
they got thin. "If we don't eat," they said,
and nodded wisely to each other.
"Eat! Eat!" their nursemaid shrieked
as if for her own life.
No use, they could have told her.
Their friends, the neighbor children, began to miss them.
They missed seeing them around the old neighborhood,
although the girls were there.
This was not much better,
having one's toes stepped on.
This would not do, the Fair One said.

It was a time to run away; I could not say
who said it first.
They had to pack. They had to sit
on the suitcase, it was so fat
but they were weak and thin.
This would not do—even two
pencils cannot carry
a suitcase over the world.
The only ones who do not have to pack
are kangaroos.

So they went to see the witch
who lived at the edge of the neighborhood.
She stuck her crooked face out the door
and sniffed: "Shoo! Shoo!"
They echoed this and circled on their toes
to a count of ten.
The Fair One heard the dark
sister's voice get hoarse.
"You've caught cold," she warned, but her own words
snuffled and woofed in her throat.
The night rose around them like a flower . . .
their noses knew
what they had never known.
The Dark Girl felt her thighs start
as if the moon pulled at them for music.
She leapt. The night light flared
in the pale hairs of her flank.
"You're beautiful!" the Fair One told the Dark,
and saw that she was too.
How they trampled the neighborhood!
The crushed grass under their paws
released its wild, sweet smells.
Their tails flattened a wake in the matted kudzu.
The wind nuzzled them in fields of fur.
Back and forth the tree frogs swung on their hinge
as if the night were a porch to a deeper night.

If only they had run away with dawn!
If only Mrs. Brown
had not put down her coffee cup
and Mr. Brown the news
and stared like children from the kitchen window
at their clothesline and the underwear in trees
and called the man who waved his silly net.

What Father said, I think, need not be said;
long ago the girls had wisely learned
when to keep out of his way. But it is said
that he takes Mother to the zoo on Sundays
with the new children. Mother says, "Now, dear,"
when Father loses his hat to the blowaway wind
and the babies chase it shrieking down the hill.
Father tries to be good. He stands at the cage
watching the marsupials and murmurs,
"I wonder." If the girls know how to get home
they're not saying or they haven't tried
or else they've tried.
Their best friends are the Chinese bears next door;
they share brown chips from a bag labeled *Omnivore*.

I DREAMT THE LOUISIANA HERON

I dreamt the Louisiana heron pitched
down again and the slate wing dropped
on the white breast where I looked up
as if a hot star had ceased, as if a piece
of deep sky broke off and tacked
into its own wind, slacked, the neck
sprouting like a stalk, the legs
like twigs planted in the brack
the sun had buffed.

STILL WINDS

What wind creases the water,
what boat divides
now that my paddle
cuts so deep?

The trawler fine as a ghost,
the merest water,
a flake of daylight moon
over the fairheaded oats.

The color cannot settle
flush with the marsh
but like a child's drawing
rides free of form.

Grass ridden by green,
volatile lizard,
an oboe rises from the nest of herons.
I'm here and there.

ISAAC CANNOT RISE FROM
THE BEAUTY OF HIS DEATHBED

The hunt was in the sky,
the tinctures of the clouds
in my father's robes.

(Tents of sleep still
scarved my mother from me.)
Deep between the ridges

of camels we rode,
then on light horses
rose into the mountains.

I carried the wood
to praise such a world
with the crisp of bonfires.

My steep father
who could lift and catch me
lifted me

from the horse to the ledge.
I looked down on the
valley of psalms.

(Mother, will you weep
an oasis
as once

when you sang
a spring
rose in your throat?)

How should I know
peace from the sword?
The day I died

even the scythe sighed
above the red wheat;
said, *clarity*; said,
the beauty of the morning.

JAMES AGEE, YOU HAVE BROKEN

James Agee, you have broken my step,
afflicted me with patience,
worn me to the largo of your breath.

You come with the sudden
intake of evening, the rill of cool
split from the melon, to sit

beneath the branch of the magnolia
which has snared
bits of a cotillion.

You accept the violet
shadows in your shirt
and cigarette papers.

(*South, I have wounds
for all your cotton.*)

Your ear to the maracus
of the deep woods,
you draw

gold from the moon,
silver from the cricket,
mercury from the drops of night.

RELIEF OF CHILDREN

for George, Richard and Thomas Morrison

The galloping oats parted;
the dune knelt down,
and they debarked in the mild forgiveness
of his dromedary eyes.
They wept to say goodbye.
How they'd loved his shaggy knees!
And as they loved, so they forgot.
The land stood up; if land can sigh,
it raised a promontory
and there they made a lookout of his grave.

They were etched children, they were spectral.
They were the article of my eye.
They ransacked cans and bottles
for messages.
They flourished their arms.
They held themselves beyond ransom.
They were taut
as the quaver of afternoon.
They stunned the tambourine of insects.

The little one,
the one with the marmalade hair,
about whose soft nape
the wind wrapped,
straddled the crest in a penny's worth of thought.
He saw the waterlight as it had leapt
from his skateblades to the ice
and back the year he saved the town.
It was a port like this, but cold.
Spars and steeples poked the stars in heaven.
And with this charm
he defended it against
the story of harm:
at low tide the sea is land,
at high tide the land is sea.

The one
who made a daddy longlegs of the sun.

The child who could read
the ways of the giraffe in palm trees.
The brow that grazes the lintel of the clouds
bowed down to her—
he who ruminates on the whispers
of the uppermost leaves.
She laid her hand on the leaf-shadowed flank
and felt the pace
of the narrative of the creatures,
never told to man.

The one
who in his nightly ascension could become
a rivet in Orion's belt.

The one who tossed
on the storm horse of a psychosis.
Oh bitter is the porridge
of knowledge.

Camp followers,
circus veterans,
raised from pink dust and shall return—

I heard them say their parts.
I tracked the five-toed fossil.
My throat hurt
in the old place where my tonsils were.
When the peacock nested in the evening sky,
I gathered the kindling;
I counted nimble sticks.
I saw the antics climb the bar,
the quarter-notes dance:
shrilling, treble children and sloe-eyed altos,
children deafened by the dissonance of families.

Why do you toil
to fill the moat
when the ocean sifts the shore
at your knee?

May vitamin and mineral uphold you,
who dig for rust
and publish gold.

SONG

Who lives on the pink horn, the lining?
Who lugs his dreams up
out of the slag of low tide
and wakes in the fish smell from the factories?

Who is the skate bug
on the patina of waters?
Who broke through the tarnish?

Who dresses by the light
of his own gray face
and starts his day in a life
full of transparencies?

Who climbs high and tiny
amid the power lines?
Who is precarious on the horizon?

Who swills the grease
and stokes his stomach with coffee
but clangs anyway
like a silver pail at his thigh?

Whose side is pierced by a train whistle?
Who is baggage in the empty freight cars
and an echo off the oil drums
deluded with rainbows?

Whose word is trespass?
Who has no friction with the day?
Whose ghost does the chimney emit?

And who'll see them home?
Who'll see they never fall
into the sun?
Who'll lick the vanilla from the clapboard?

Who'll stake their claim to the margin?
Who hears them
reverberate with sunset?

I. I will. I am.
Life is wasted
on me.

I'll mind the stoop.
I'll shuck dusk
from the oyster
and drain it of warm rain.

I sniff the heady trash fires.
I have my light
in shadow.

But I know evening is a guitar
and I'll take it in my arms.
I'll lay our songs across it.

We'll watch our sky
grow tense again and listen
along the ledge
for the same birds, the old words.

The National Poetry Series

First Annual Series— 1980

Winner of the Open Competition:

Wendy Salinger, *Folly River* (selected by Donald Hall)

Other Winners:

Sterling A. Brown, *Collected Poems* (selected by Michael Harper)

Joseph Langland, *Any Body's Song* (selected by Ann Stanford)

Ronald Perry, *Denizens* (selected by Donald Justice)

Roberta Spear, *Silk* (selected by Philip Levine)